W9-AGA-372

Hokie Bird's Journey Through Virginia

Aimee Aryal

Virginia Tech Class of 1993

Illustrated by Gerry Perez

Virginia Tech Class of 2002

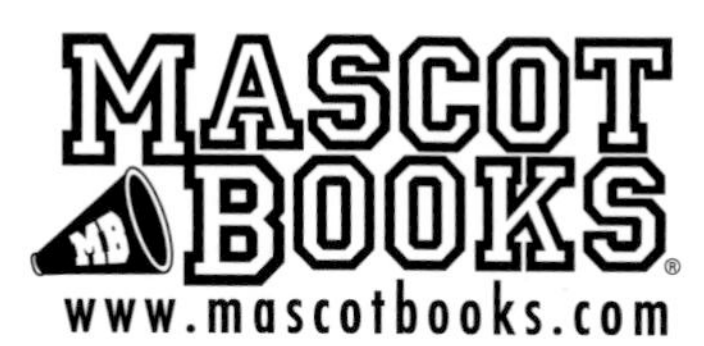

Burruss Hall is the main administrative building at Virginia Tech and was constructed in 1936.

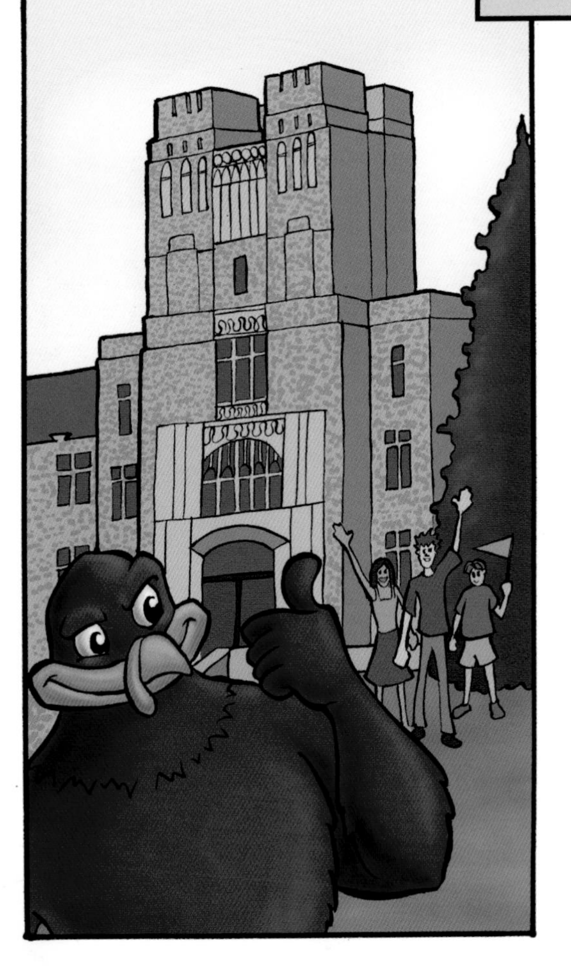

Hokie Bird was enjoying a relaxing summer on the campus of Virginia Tech. With football season fast approaching, Hokie Bird decided to take one last summer vacation. He thought it would be great fun to take a journey throughout the Commonwealth of Virginia, where he could see interesting places and make new friends along the way.

Blacksburg, Virginia is the proud home of Virginia Polytechnic Institute and State University.
WELCOME TO BLACKSBURG
VT

Before hitting the road, Hokie Bird stopped at Burruss Hall and the Duck Pond to tell his friends about his vacation plans. "Goodbye, Hokie Bird! Have a nice trip!" said his fans. The mascot packed his bags, hopped into the Hokie Mobile, and hit the road!

Southwest Virginia is known for its coal mines and dairy farms.

Hokie Bird's first stop was nearby Southwest Virginia. He dressed in special mining equipment and headed deep down into a coal mine. It sure was dark down there!

Hokie Bird then took a tour of a dairy farm, where he learned how to milk a cow! The cow mooed, "Hello, Hokie Bird!"

Hokie Bird made a stop in Hillsville, Virginia, the hometown of Virginia Tech football coach, Frank Beamer. Coach Beamer was happy to see Hokie Bird in Hillsville. He said, "Hello, Hokie Bird!"

Coach Beamer graduated from V.P.I. in 1969 and is the winningest football coach in the history of Virginia Tech.

Hokie Bird continued to Roanoke, Virginia. Wanting to be well-rested for the remainder of his trip, Hokie Bird checked in to the luxurious and historic Hotel Roanoke. As he arrived at the hotel, Hokie Bird was given a hero's welcome by the hotel staff. They cheered, "Hello, Hokie Bird!"

Hokie Bird had one more stop to make in Roanoke. He drove the Hokie Mobile atop Mill Mountain to see Roanoke's Star, the city's most recognizable landmark.

Roanoke is nicknamed
"The Star City of the South."

Lee Chapel is named for Robert E. Lee and was completed in 1868.

The campus of VMI is referred to as the "Post."

From Roanoke, Hokie Bird made the short drive north on I-81 to Lexington, Virginia. On the campus of Washington & Lee University, Hokie Bird snapped a picture of historic Lee Chapel. From W&L, Hokie Bird made his way to the Parade Grounds at Virginia Military Institute. Hokie Bird proudly marched with the VMI Cadets. The cadets cheered, "Hello, Hokie Bird!"

From Lexington, Hokie Bird drove the Hokie Mobile east on I-64 to Charlottesville, Virginia, home to another Virginia university. As Hokie Bird walked through campus, he started to feel a little uncomfortable. Fortunately, he spotted a Virginia Tech fan nearby and raced to greet him. The Tech fan called, "Hokie, Hokie, Hokie, Hi, Hokie Bird!"

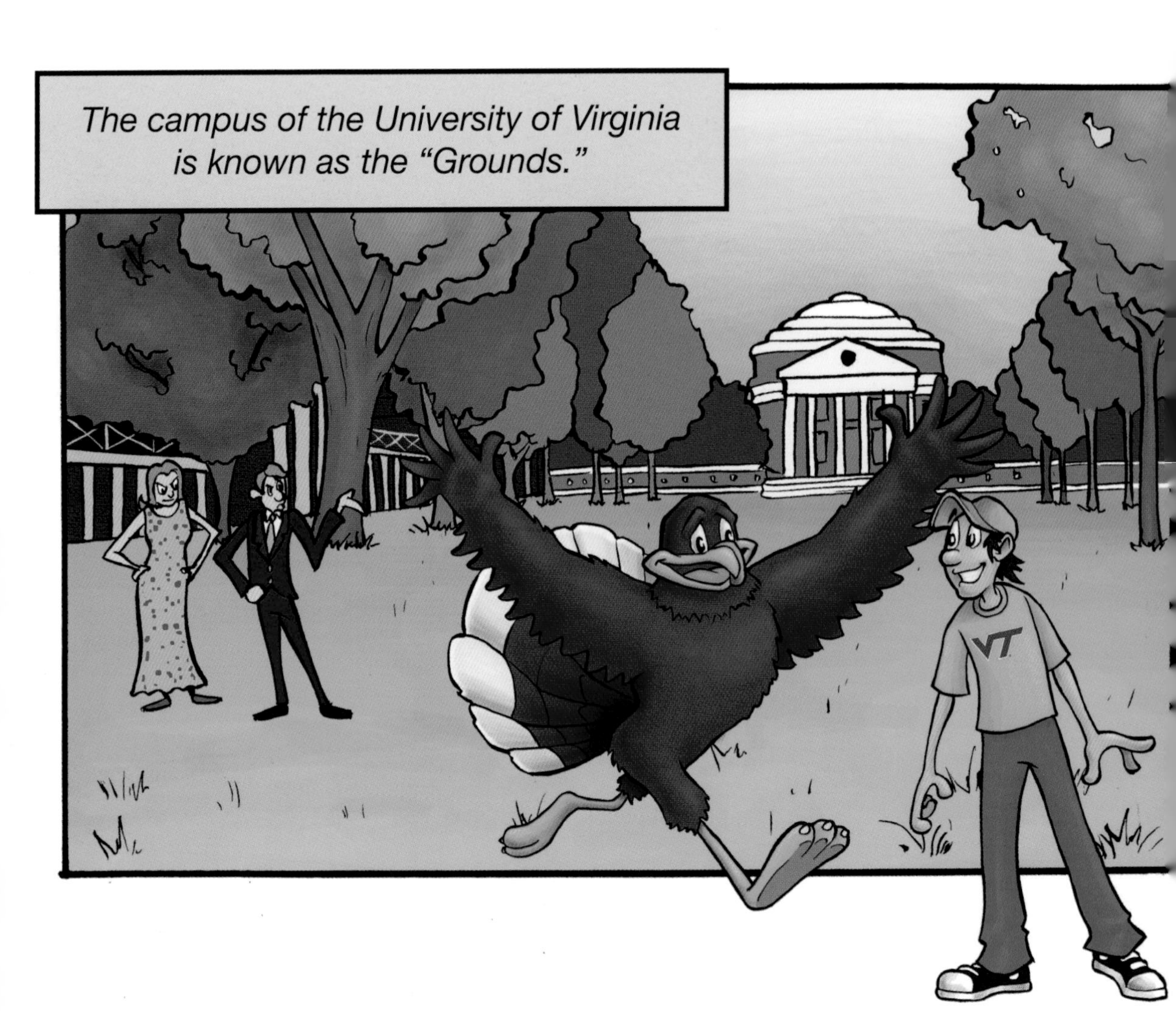

The campus of the University of Virginia is known as the "Grounds."
VT

Hokie Bird then traveled to Monticello, home of Thomas Jefferson. Hokie Bird was excited to learn about Jefferson's amazing accomplishments as he imagined what life at Monticello would have been like over two hundred years ago.

Monticello was the home of Thomas Jefferson, the third President of the United States of America, and author of the Declaration of Independence. "Monticello" is Italian for "little mountain."

Next, it was on to Virginia's Shenandoah Mountains. Hokie Bird laced up his hiking boots, found a perfect walking stick, and headed down a trail. From the mountains, Hokie Bird looked down at the beautiful Shenandoah Valley. After taking a couple wrong turns, he found himself at one of the many poultry farms in the area. Hokie Bird thought, "Yikes!" as he raced out of the coop.

Poultry farming is a major industry in the Shenandoah Valley.

Shenandoah National Park has over 500 miles of hiking trails.
Looking for a safe place to hide, Hokie Bird made it to Luray Caverns. He took a tour of the caverns and learned all about how the rocks and caverns were formed.
Luray Caverns is one of the most popular tourist destinations in Virginia with over 500,000 visitors annually.

Hokie Bird took I-66 into Northern Virginia. He visited many Virginia Tech fans and alumni in the area. He was excited to go shopping at Tysons Corner. As he headed to the mall, Hokie Bird found himself in bumper-to-bumper traffic. Hokie Bird wasn't used to this kind of traffic!

After an afternoon of shopping, it was time to go sightseeing. Hokie Bird toured Fairfax, Old Town Alexandria, and Arlington. He even crossed the Potomac River into Washington, D.C. and visited the White House, the Washington Monument, and the United States Capitol. Everywhere he went, he ran into Virginia Tech fans cheering, "Hello, Hokie Bird!"

Approximately 2,000,000 people live in Northern Virginia, about one-fourth of the state's total population. Nearly 40,000 Virginia Tech alumni live in Northern Virginia.

Robert E. Lee, J.E.B. Stuart, Jefferson Davis, Stonewall Jackson, Matthew Fontaine Maury, and Arthur Ashe are honored along Monument Avenue in Richmond.

It was time to head south on I-95 to Richmond, the capital city of the Commonwealth of Virginia. Hokie Bird ran into politicians outside the Capitol Building. The politicians cheered, “Hello, Hokie Bird!” Next, Hokie Bird took a stroll down historic Monument Avenue, where he admired the statues of famous Virginians.

Ready for some thrills, Hokie Bird took the Hokie Mobile on to the racetrack in Richmond. He zoomed around the track! Race fans cheered, “Go, Hokie Bird, go!”

Colonial Williamsburg is a restored 18th-century British settlement.

Hokie Bird's next stop was Williamsburg, Virginia. In Colonial Williamsburg, Hokie Bird changed into his colonial clothing and participated in a reenactment of daily life in a British settlement. "You're such a fine gentleman, Hokie Bird," said a young lady.

After a day of visiting historic landmarks, it was time for the mascot to hit the golf course. Hokie Bird teed off at a nearby golf course with a perfect shot. His playing partners cheered, "Nice shot, Hokie Bird!"

Finally, Hokie Bird headed to Busch Gardens and rode a roller coaster. "Go, Hokie Bird, go!" shouted his friends.

Williamsburg is home to
many beautiful golf courses.
VT

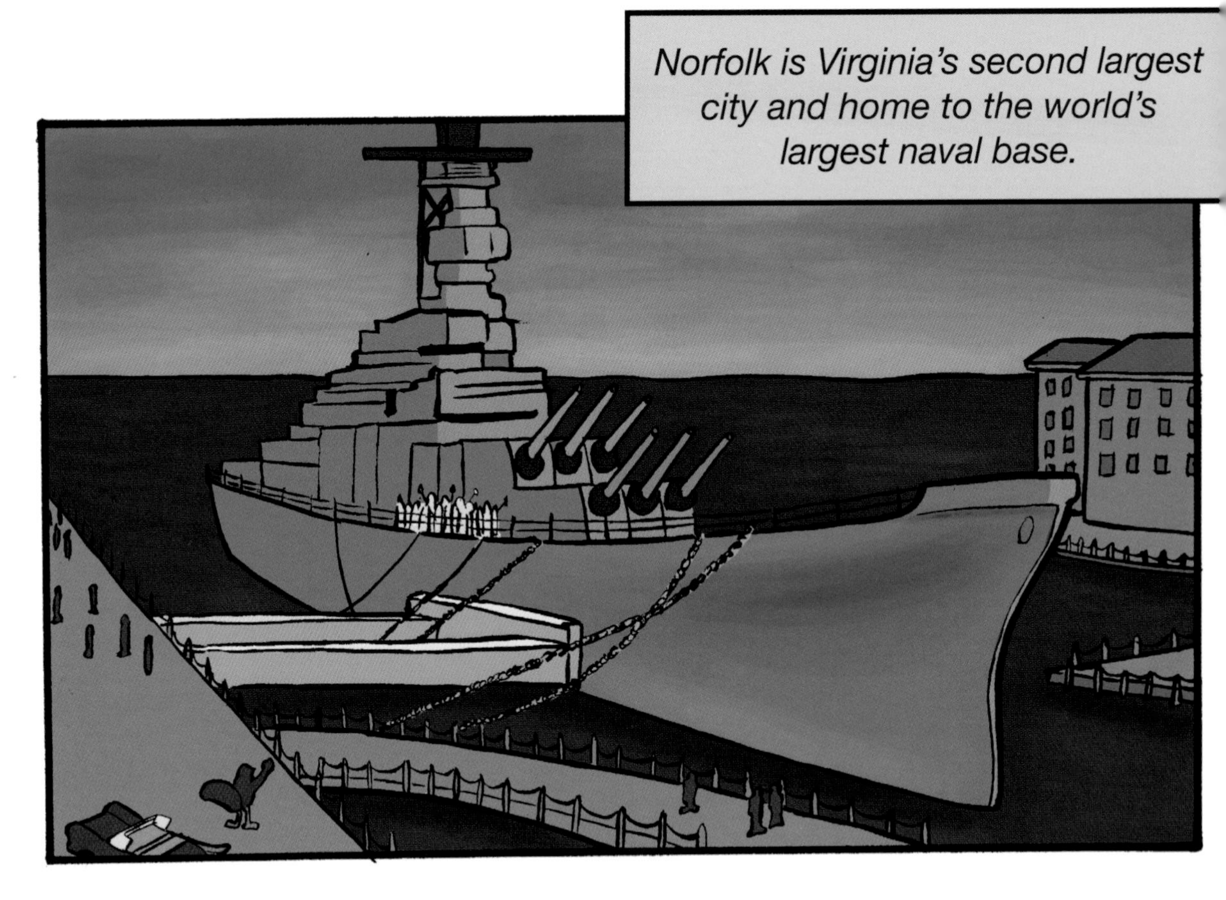

Hokie Bird continued east on I-64, stopping next at Norfolk, Virginia. Hokie Bird had heard all about the amazing ships docked in Norfolk so he wanted to take a look for himself. Hokie Bird imagined himself taking the helm and leading a faithful crew all over the world.

However, the ship's captain had another job for Hokie Bird. He was handed a mop and bucket and directed to scrub the deck!

As Hokie Bird worked away, other sailors on the ship teased, "Scrub, Hokie Bird, scrub!"

After all that hard work, Hokie Bird was ready to relax on the beach. At Virginia Beach, he built a sandcastle, swam in the ocean, and soaked up the sun.

Hokie Bird fell asleep on the beach and started dreaming about the upcoming football season. He couldn't wait to see all his friends and fans back in Blacksburg in the fall. Hokie Bird was ready to start his journey home.

Tysons
Corner

Finally, Hokie Bird made it back to Blacksburg, Virginia. What a great vacation it had been! Once back on campus, Hokie Bird was greeted by many Hokie fans. They cheered, “Hello, Hokie Bird! Welcome home!”

For my little Hokies, Anna and Maya, and all their little Hokie friends. ~ Aimee Aryal

For Amrit, Tuan, Dom, Jordan, Tom, Jon, Richie, Rana, Professor Graham and all my fellow Hokies out there. ~ Gerry Perez

For more information about our products, please visit us online at www.mascotbooks.com.

For more information, please contact Mascot Books,
P.O. Box 220157, Chantilly, VA 20153-0157

ISBN: 1-932888-69-1
Printed in the United States.

www.mascotbooks.com

Title List

Baseball

Team	Title	Author
Boston Red Sox	Hello, Wally!	Jerry Remy
Boston Red Sox	Wally And His Journey Through Red Sox Nation!	Jerry Remy
Boston Red Sox	Coast to Coast with Wally	Jerry Remy
Boston Red Sox	A Season with Wally	Jerry Remy
Colorado Rockies	Hello, Dinger!	Aimee Aryal
Detroit Tigers	Hello, Paws!	Aimee Aryal
New York Yankees	Let's Go, Yankees!	Yogi Berra
New York Yankees	Yankees Town	Aimee Aryal
New York Mets	Hello, Mr. Met!	Rusty Staub
New York Mets	Mr. Met and his Journey Through the Big Apple	Aimee Aryal
St. Louis Cardinals	Hello, Fredbird!	Ozzie Smith
Philadelphia Phillies	Hello, Phillie Phanatic!	Aimee Aryal
Chicago Cubs	Let's Go, Cubs!	Aimee Aryal
Chicago White Sox	Let's Go, White Sox!	Aimee Aryal
Cleveland Indians	Hello, Slider!	Bob Feller
Seattle Mariners	Hello, Mariner Moose!	Aimee Aryal
Washington Nationals	Hello, Screech!	Aimee Aryal
Milwaukee Brewers	Hello Bernie Brewer!	Aimee Aryal

Pro Football

Team	Title	Author
Carolina Panthers	Let's Go, Panthers!	Aimee Aryal
Chicago Bears	Let's Go, Bears!	Aimee Aryal
Dallas Cowboys	How 'Bout Them Cowboys!	Aimee Aryal
Green Bay Packers	Go, Pack, Go!	Aimee Aryal
Kansas City Chiefs	Let's Go, Chiefs!	Aimee Aryal
Minnesota Vikings	Let's Go, Vikings!	Aimee Aryal
New York Giants	Let's Go, Giants!	Aimee Aryal
New York Jets	J-E-T-S! Jets, Jets, Jets!	Aimee Aryal
New England Patriots	Let's Go, Patriots!	Aimee Aryal
Seattle Seahawks	Let's Go, Seahawks!	Aimee Aryal
Washington Redskins	Hail To The Redskins!	Aimee Aryal

Basketball

Team	Title	Author
Dallas Mavericks	Let's Go, Mavs!	Mark Cuban
Boston Celtics	Let's Go, Celtics!	Aimee Aryal

Other

Event	Title	Author
Kentucky Derby	White Diamond Runs For The Roses	Aimee Aryal
Marine Corps Marathon	Run, Miles, Run!	Aimee Aryal

College

School	Title	Author
Alabama	Hello, Big Al!	Aimee Aryal
Alabama	Roll Tide!	Ken Stabler
Alabama	Big Al's Journey Through the Yellowhammer State	Aimee Aryal
Arizona	Hello, Wilbur!	Lute Olson
Arkansas	Hello, Big Red!	Aimee Aryal
Arkansas	Big Red's Journey Through the Razorback State	Aimee Aryal
Auburn	Hello, Aubie!	Aimee Aryal
Auburn	War Eagle!	Pat Dye
Auburn	Aubie's Journey Through the Yellowhammer State	Aimee Aryal
Boston College	Hello, Baldwin!	Aimee Aryal
Brigham Young	Hello, Cosmo!	LaVell Edwards
Cal - Berkeley	Hello, Oski!	Aimee Aryal
Clemson	Hello, Tiger!	Aimee Aryal
Clemson	Tiger's Journey Through the Palmetto State	Aimee Aryal
Colorado	Hello, Ralphie!	Aimee Aryal
Connecticut	Hello, Jonathan!	Aimee Aryal
Duke	Hello, Blue Devil!	Aimee Aryal
Florida	Hello, Albert!	Aimee Aryal
Florida	Albert's Journey Through the Sunshine State	Aimee Aryal
Florida State	Let's Go, 'Noles!	Aimee Aryal
Georgia	Hello, Hairy Dawg!	Aimee Aryal
Georgia	How 'Bout Them Dawgs!	Vince Dooley
Georgia	Hairy Dawg's Journey Through the Peach State	Vince Dooley
Georgia Tech	Hello, Buzz!	Aimee Aryal
Gonzaga	Spike, The Gonzaga Bulldog	Mike Pringle
Illinois	Let's Go, Illini!	Aimee Aryal
Indiana	Let's Go, Hoosiers!	Aimee Aryal
Iowa	Hello, Herky!	Aimee Aryal
Iowa State	Hello, Cy!	Amy DeLashmutt
James Madison	Hello, Duke Dog!	Aimee Aryal
Kansas	Hello, Big Jay!	Aimee Aryal
Kansas State	Hello, Willie!	Dan Walter
Kentucky	Hello, Wildcat!	Aimee Aryal
LSU	Hello, Mike!	Aimee Aryal
LSU	Mike's Journey Through the Bayou State	Aimee Aryal
Maryland	Hello, Testudo!	Aimee Aryal
Michigan	Let's Go, Blue!	Aimee Aryal
Michigan State	Hello, Sparty!	Aimee Aryal
Minnesota	Hello, Goldy!	Aimee Aryal
Mississippi	Hello, Colonel Rebel!	Aimee Aryal
Mississippi State	Hello, Bully!	Aimee Aryal
Missouri	Hello, Truman!	Todd Donoho
Nebraska	Hello, Herbie Husker!	Aimee Aryal
North Carolina	Hello, Rameses!	Aimee Aryal
North Carolina	Rameses' Journey Through the Tar Heel State	Aimee Aryal
North Carolina St.	Hello, Mr. Wuf!	Aimee Aryal
North Carolina St.	Mr. Wuf's Journey Through North Carolina	Aimee Aryal
Notre Dame	Let's Go, Irish!	Aimee Aryal
Ohio State	Hello, Brutus!	Aimee Aryal
Ohio State	Brutus' Journey	Aimee Aryal
Oklahoma	Let's Go, Sooners!	Aimee Aryal
Oklahoma State	Hello, Pistol Pete!	Aimee Aryal
Oregon	Let's Go Ducks!	Aimee Aryal
Oregon State	Hello, Benny the Beaver!	Aimee Aryal
Penn State	Hello, Nittany Lion!	Aimee Aryal
Penn State	We Are Penn State!	Joe Paterno
Purdue	Hello, Purdue Pete!	Aimee Aryal
Rutgers	Hello, Scarlet Knight!	Aimee Aryal
South Carolina	Hello, Cocky!	Aimee Aryal
South Carolina	Cocky's Journey Through the Palmetto State	Aimee Aryal
So. California	Hello, Tommy Trojan!	Aimee Aryal
Syracuse	Hello, Otto!	Aimee Aryal
Tennessee	Hello, Smokey!	Aimee Aryal
Tennessee	Smokey's Journey Through the Volunteer State	Aimee Aryal
Texas	Hello, Hook 'Em!	Aimee Aryal
Texas	Hook 'Em's Journey Through the Lone Star State	Aimee Aryal
Texas A & M	Howdy, Reveille!	Aimee Aryal
Texas A & M	Reveille's Journey Through the Lone Star State	Aimee Aryal
Texas Tech	Hello, Masked Rider!	Aimee Aryal
UCLA	Hello, Joe Bruin!	Aimee Aryal
Virginia	Hello, CavMan!	Aimee Aryal
Virginia Tech	Hello, Hokie Bird!	Aimee Aryal
Virginia Tech	Yea, It's Hokie Game Day!	Frank Beamer
Virginia Tech	Hokie Bird's Journey Through Virginia	Aimee Aryal
Wake Forest	Hello, Demon Deacon!	Aimee Aryal
Washington	Hello, Harry the Husky!	Aimee Aryal
Washington State	Hello, Butch!	Aimee Aryal
West Virginia	Hello, Mountaineer!	Aimee Aryal
Wisconsin	Hello, Bucky!	Aimee Aryal
Wisconsin	Bucky's Journey Through the Badger State	Aimee Aryal

Order online at **mascotbooks.com** using promo code " **free**" to receive **FREE SHIPPING**!

More great titles coming soon!

info@mascotbooks.com

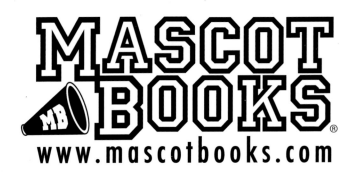

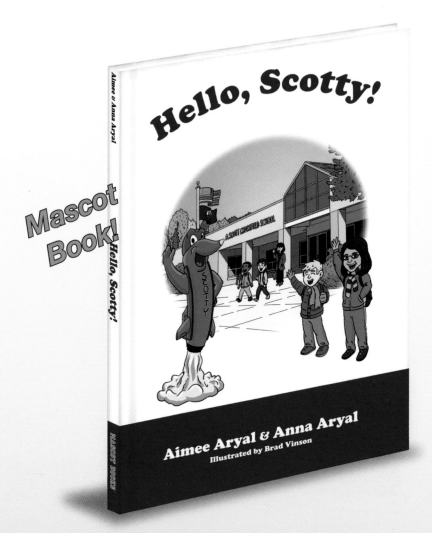